A gift to

_____

From

_____

On this awesome day

_____

Father to the fatherless,
defender of widows—
this is God, whose dwelling is holy.
God places the lonely in families.
—PSALM 68:5–6 NLT

Dedication

To my dear, gruff daddy, Everett Andrew Harper,
who didn't get to meet Missy before he died but
tenderly asked, "When is our girl coming home?"
right before slipping into the arms of Jesus.

The Scripture marked CSB is taken from the Christian Standard Bible®,
Copyright © 2017 by Holman Bible Publishers. Used by permission. Christian
Standard Bible® and CSB® are federally registered trademarks of Holman Bible
Publishers. Scriptures marked NLT are taken from Holy Bible, New Living
Translation, copyright © 1996, 2004, 2015 by Tyndale House Foundation.
Used by permission of Tyndale House Publishers, Inc., Carol Stream, Illinois 60188.
All rights reserved.

DEWEY: C306.874 SUBHD: GOD/FATHERS/PARENT-CHILD RELATIONSHIP

Printed in Shenzhen, Guangdong, China in June 2018

1 2 3 4 5 6 · 22 21 20 19 18

WHO's Your Daddy?

Discovering the Awesomest Daddy Ever

Lisa and Missy Harper

Illustrated by Olivia Duchess

B&H KIDS

Nashville, Tennessee

Hi, my name is Missy, but sometimes my mom calls me Toots, Punkin', Peanut, or Squirty McTurty. I'm adopted, I like to swim, and I love cheese sticks!

5

For as long as I can remember, it's just been me and Mommy and Cookie the Wonder Dog living at our house.

I always thought our family was perfect, until one day in kindergarten, George asked me a question....

"Who's your daddy?"

I thought about it a minute and said, "I don't have one." But George made a scrunchy face and tilted his head to one side like he was confused.

"But I thought everybody has a daddy! Who plays soccer with you and drives you to school and makes pancakes for you?"

Then the teacher told us to stop talking, so I just put my head down and started coloring.

That afternoon when Mommy picked me up from school, I told her about George's question. She put her chin in her hand, which is what she does when she's thinking real hard, and drove us to the park near my school. When we reached the pond, she turned around and said, "Come here, baby," and let me sit in her lap.

After she played with my hair for a few minutes—which makes me feel happy and safe and sleepy all at the same time—she said, "Honey, you actually do have a Daddy, and His name is Daddy God. He knew you before you were born, and He loves you more than all the stars in the sky."

I thought about that on the way to the grocery store.
Then I asked Mommy, "If God is my Daddy, how come He doesn't drive me to school or teach me to play soccer or make me pancakes like George's daddy?"

She responded, "Well, sweetie, Daddy God is invisible, so we can't see Him the way we can see human daddies with skin on. And even though Daddy God doesn't drive a car, coach soccer, or make pancakes, He did create the whole, wide world, and He is always with you and He will never, ever leave you and will never, ever stop loving you."

15

When we got to the grocery store, I had lots of questions.

"Is God everyone's Daddy?" I asked while we put mangos (my most favorite fruit ever) in our cart.

"Yes," she answered, "but some people don't know He's their heavenly Father yet."

"So kids who have skin daddies get Daddy God too?" I asked.

"Yes, they do," Mommy said with a smile.

"But if they already have a skin daddy why do they need God to be their Daddy?" I wondered out loud while skipping down the aisle.

"Even though skin daddies are wonderful, Toots, they aren't perfect like Daddy God. Remember how I was impatient with you the other night and apologized for raising my voice? Well, skin mommies and daddies make mistakes sometimes.

"Plus, see that skin daddy right over there? He's a soldier, and sometimes soldiers have to go far, far away to work and don't get to come home for a long, long time."

I thought and thought about skin daddies and Daddy God on the way home. It was definitely going to take a while to figure this whole dad thing out! By the time we got home, I had another question. . . .

Mommy + me

"Mommy, do skin daddies who go away always come back?"

I could tell it was what Mommy calls "a whopper of a question" because she tilted her head to the side just like George had when I told him I didn't have a daddy. Then she stopped putting away the groceries and said, "Come here, Punkin'" and led me to the swing on our front porch.

We swung back and forth for a few minutes and watched a rabbit scamper across the yard before Mommy replied softly, "Sweetheart, some skin daddies don't come back home to their kids, and some skin mommies don't get to either."

She reminded me of how my first mommy, Mama Marie, loved me with her whole heart but got super sick in Haiti and had to leave me when she went to heaven.

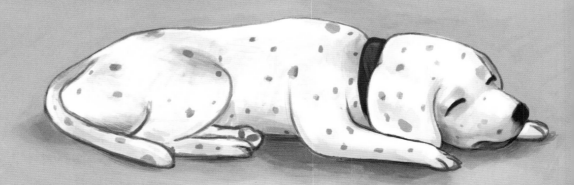

We talked about how Mama Marie's death makes me sad, and then we talked about another really sad thing called divorce. Mommy told me divorce is when husbands and wives grow hurt sticks on their hearts and stop living together because they keep poking each other.

When I said that it was definitely going to take a while to figure out why death and divorce make us so sad, she chuckled and said, "Oh, baby, you don't have to figure it all out now."

"When you're sad, just scoot as close as you can to Daddy God and tell Him everything that's on your heart." Then she wrapped her skin arms around me and said to imagine Daddy God's great big arms around both of us. And pretty soon I didn't feel sad at all anymore.

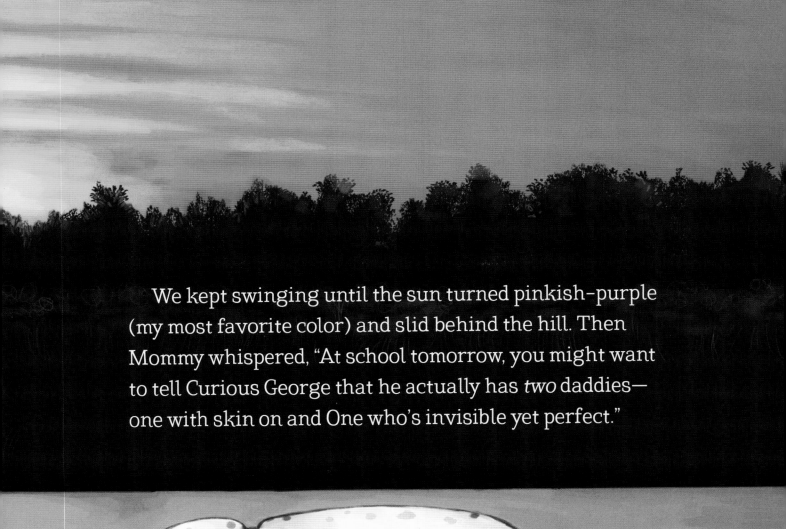

We kept swinging until the sun turned pinkish-purple (my most favorite color) and slid behind the hill. Then Mommy whispered, "At school tomorrow, you might want to tell Curious George that he actually has *two* daddies— one with skin on and One who's invisible yet perfect."

Which is exactly what I did the next day . . . well, actually, I told my *whole* class about Daddy God, the awesomest Daddy ever. Because when you figure out something this good, you just can't keep it to yourself!

Remember:

"Father to the fatherless, defender of widows—this is God, whose dwelling is holy. God places the lonely in families."—Psalm 68:5–6 NLT

Read:

Read 1 John 3:1. This verse tells us that Father God's love for us is so great that He calls us all His sons and daughters. The Bible talks continuously about God as Father, how He watches over us without sleep and loves us without end. He is the role model for all earthly parents as we strive to guide our little ones. But many children do not know the consistent love of a father here on earth. Thankfully, even if their parents are lost or absent, children can be comforted by knowing they are loved by the all-powerful Father, the one from whom every family is named (Ephesians 3:15 CSB). They only need to know and soak in this incredible love.

After reading this book, please consider reading Psalm 139:1–18 from a children's Bible to further explain to your children the permanence of their Daddy God.

Think:

1. Missy called daddies here on earth "skin daddies." Can you name three awesome things about this kind of daddy? (If your child's biological father isn't in their life, prompt them to share what they think would be great about a human dad.)

2. How are "skin daddies" different from Daddy God? How are they alike?

3. Missy talked to her mommy about death and divorce. Why do those things make us sad? Why are they sometimes hard to think about?

4. If you could see Daddy God right now, would you run up and hug Him or hide and act shy? (If your child says they'd act shy, gently prompt them to explain why they wouldn't feel comfortable hugging or being hugged by God.)

5. Missy was excited to tell her class about Daddy God, the awesomest Daddy ever. What are your three favorite things about Him?